This
SpongeBob SquarePants
Annual belongs to:

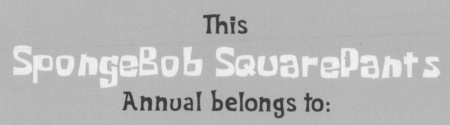

Ollie ~~Heath~~ Colgan

SpongeBob SquarePants™

ANNUAL 2008

CONTENTS

Edited by Brenda Apsley   Designed by Graham Wise

EGMONT
We bring stories to life

First published in Great Britain in 2007 by Egmont UK Limited,
239 Kensington High Street, London W8 6SA. All rights reserved.

ISBN 978 1 4052 3174 9
1 3 5 7 9 10 8 6 4 2
Printed in Italy.

SPONGEBOB SQUAREPANTS

BIKINI ATOLL is an island in the Pacific Ocean. Far down in the depths is the underwater city of BIKINI BOTTOM. You won't find it on any map or chart, but it's there all right. You'll find shops, restaurants, a launderette and even a boating lake – everything you need for a life underwater!

Bikini Bottom's most famous inhabitant is SPONGEBOB SQUAREPANTS. He's a yellow sea sponge who lives in a two-bedroom home shaped just like a PINEAPPLE ... When his super-loud foghorn alarm clock goes off –

HONNNNKKKKK!

– it's the start of another spongy day!

8

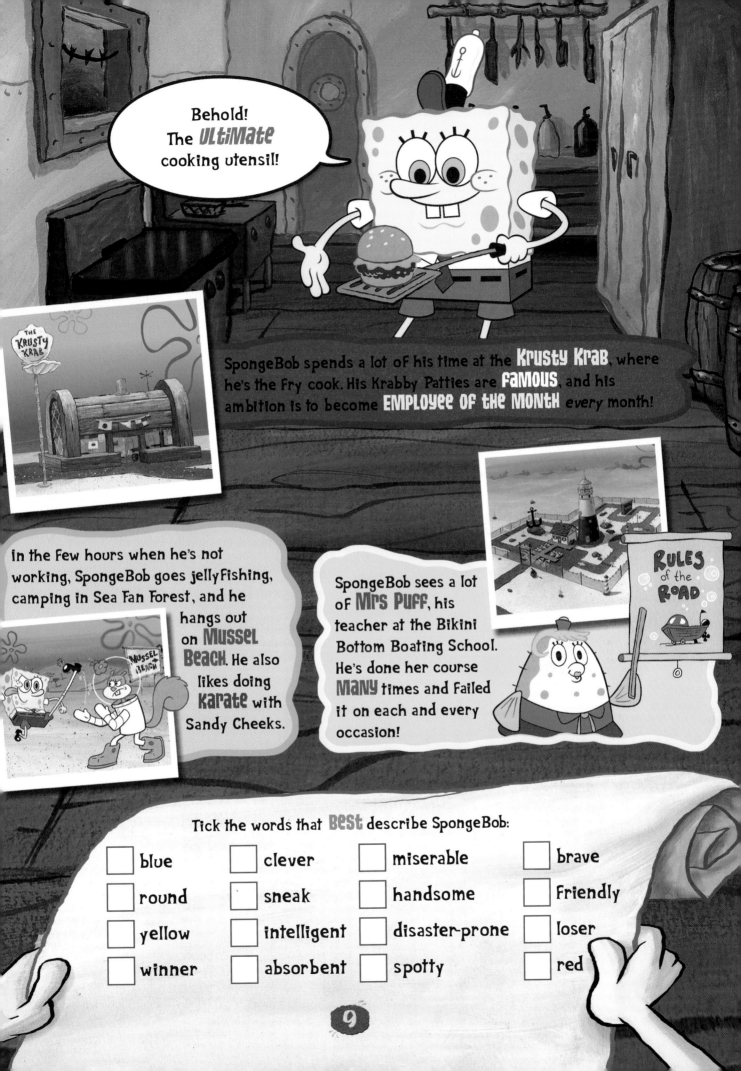

Behold! The **ULTiMATE** cooking utensil!

SpongeBob spends a lot of his time at the **Krusty Krab**, where he's the Fry cook. His Krabby Patties are **FAMOUS**, and his ambition is to become **EMPLOYEE OF THE MONTH** every month!

In the Few hours when he's not working, SpongeBob goes jellyFishing, camping in Sea Fan Forest, and he hangs out on **MUSSEL BEACH**. He also likes doing **KARATE** with Sandy Cheeks.

SpongeBob sees a lot of **Mrs Puff**, his teacher at the Bikini Bottom Boating School. He's done her course **MANY** times and Failed it on each and every occasion!

Tick the words that **BEST** describe SpongeBob:

☐ blue	☐ clever	☐ miserable	☐ brave
☐ round	☐ sneak	☐ handsome	☐ Friendly
☐ yellow	☐ intelligent	☐ disaster-prone	☐ loser
☐ winner	☐ absorbent	☐ spotty	☐ red

Gary

Gary is SpongeBob's pet snail. He's not exactly cuddly (he's slimy if we're being truthful) and he doesn't have anything to say for himself except, "Meow!"

Having said that, Gary is not without talents ... One of them is tying SHOELACES.

He can also be a LAMP ...

pull a SLED ...

and be somewhere to hang a Hat!

SpongeBob has lots of shots of his favourite pet in his photo album.

Souped-up snail

Kissy-kissy snail

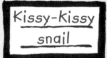

Gym buddy

Party snail

Patrick Star

What can we say about **PATRICK**? Well, not a lot, really, except that he's SpongeBob's best friend, and will do **ANYTHING** for his sea sponge buddy.

Patrick lives in the next-house-but-one to his friend, at 120 Conch Street. Passers-by may just see a rock, but to Patrick this no-mod-cons rental is home. He spends all his time there, clinging to the bottom. He doesn't have a job; where would he find the time to work between long spells of SLEEPING and lying **DORMANT** if he did?

Here's Patrick's page in SpongeBob's photo album. The labels have come unstuck. Write them in the boxes.

Turbo
Patrick

Ideas
Patrick

Party
Patrick

Action
Patrick

11

SANDY CHEEKS

SANDY CHEEKS is a squirrel from Texas. She lives in an oak tree under a glass dome called the **TREEDOME**. It's an air-bubble house, and Sandy wears a special suit so she can breathe under water. And boy, does she need to breathe ...

Sandy loves **KARATE** and going to Sand Mountain, near Mussel Beach, where she rides a chairlift to the top and zooms down on a surfboard.

SpongeBob loves hanging out with Sandy, even if it does mean wearing a **HELMET**, **ARMOUR** and a **PARACHUTE**!

These are SpongeBob's fave photos of Sandy.

KAH-RAH-TAY!

SQUIDWARD TENTACLES

SQUIDWARD TENTACLES lives next door to SpongeBob, in a house which looks like an Easter Island Head. Playing clarinet with the Bikini Bottom Philharmonic Orchestra is what he would really like to do. Problem is, he's rubbish! So he works as a waiter at the **Krusty Krab** instead.

Despite his name, Squidward is an octopus, and a rather superior one at that. He likes having his six tentacles manicured every Thursday, and conducting Beethoven.

Everything annoys him: the Krusty Krab, his customers, his boss, even SpongeBob. As he's fond of saying: **"I hate all of you!"**

Tell Squidward to **"say cheese!"** and this is what you get.

Mr Eugene Krabs

The **Krusty Krab** is the most popular fast food joint in Bikini Bottom. As its proud owner **Mr Eugene Krabs** will tell you (over and over and over again): "it's the finest eating establishment ever established for eating."

An old lobster pot, the Krusty Krab is popular because it serves SpongeBob's chargrilled **Krabby Patties**. Mr Krabs doesn't want to lose SpongeBob because he's the perfect employee: he works very hard for very long hours for very little pay.

Mr Krabs' daughter **Pearl** is the largest teenager on the planet! She's got a brain to match the size of her whale of a body, and her father hopes she'll use her maths skills to take over counting his money one day.

Gimme a **SPONGE**!
Gimme a **BOB**!
GO-O-O, **Krusty crew!**

SHELDON PLANKTON

CHUM BUCKET

CHUM BURGER

CHUM FRIES

CHUM SHAKE

CHUM ON A STICK

ORDERS

If the Krusty Krab is the finest place to eat in Bikini Bottom, the CHUM BUCKET is the worst. By a long way. By a very long way. It's so bad that no one eats there. Ever.

Its owner is SHELDON PLANKTON. He knows the only way he'll ever be successful is if he can steal the secret recipe for Krabby Patties from Mr Krabs.

He may be tiny, microscopic even, but his plots and schemes are big and bold. He carries them out with the help of his wife, a computer called KAREN.

I am SMALL!

Plankton has no friends, but a very large family. Here are a few of them. They have one thing in common: They are all GREEN.

15

Story: Kent Osborne. Layouts: Ted Couldron. Pencils: Gregg Schigiel. Inks: Jay Lender. Colour: SnoCone Studios. Lettering: Comicraft. SpongeBob SquarePants created by Stephen Hillenburg

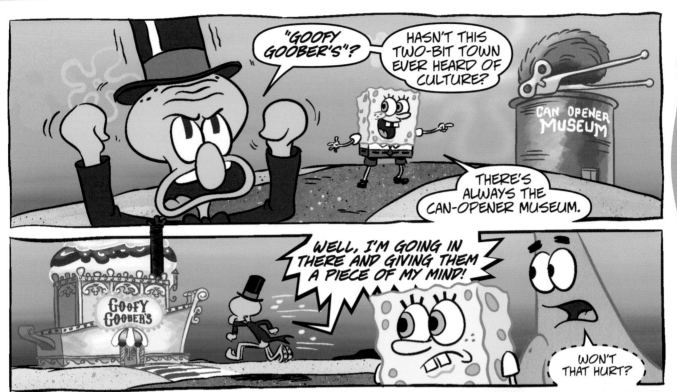

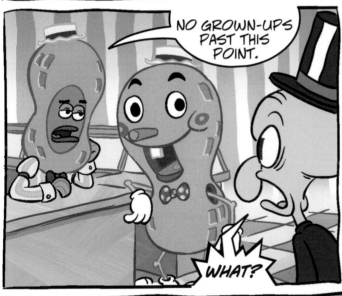

NOW WHAT DO I DO?

DON'T WORRY, SQUIDWARD! WE'LL GO IN AND GIVE THEM A PIECE OF YOUR MIND!

YEAH! WE'LL MAKE THEM REGRET MESSING WITH OUR PAL SQUIDWARD.

OKAY, MARCH RIGHT IN THERE AND TELL THEM THAT THAT NO ONE ASKED FOR THEIR *FUN RESTAURANT*, AND IF THEY *HAD* ASKED I WOULD HAVE POINTED OUT THAT NOTHING IS MORE FUN THAN BEING EXPOSED TO GREAT CULTURAL WORKS LIKE...

GOTCHA!

...AND THAT SOMETHING SO JUVENILE AS A TALKING PEANUT COULD NEVER COMPARE WITH THE SOPHISTICATED BALANCE OF WIND PERCUSSION COMBINED...

RIGHT ON!

AHEM. WE'D LIKE TO SPEAK TO THE MANAGER OF THIS ESTABLISHMENT.

RIGHT AWAY, SIR.

TICK TICK TICK TICK TICK

WELL, WE WAITED A WHOLE TEN SECONDS.

LET'S GO FIND HIM.

18

BUT ONCE INSIDE...

LOOK, SPONGEBOB! THEY HAVE STRAW HATS!

AND THEY HAVE GAMES OF CHANCE!

AND AN ANIMATRONIC JUG BAND FEATURING GOOFY GOOBER AND THE NUTTY JUNCTION CROONERS!

AND ALL THEY SERVE IS ICE CREAM!!!

YOU GENTLEMEN HAD SOMETHING TO TELL THE MANAGER?

≹AHEM≹ YES, WE DO!

YEAH, TELL HIM! TELL HIM!

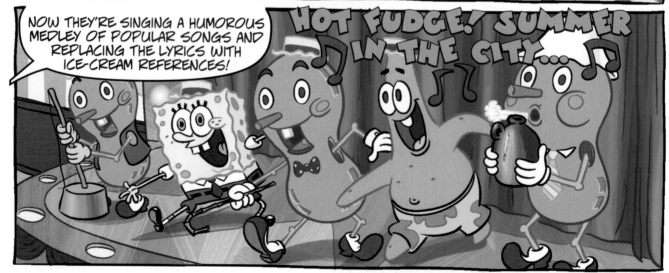

NO! NO! NO! THEY'RE SUPPOSED TO BE GIVING THEM A PIECE OF MY MIND...

...NOT GIVING IN TO...

...UH...DELICIOUS-LOOKING...UH... SCRUMPTIOUS...

...ICE CREAM!

PARENT ZONE

SLUUURP

HEY, OLD MAN, NO LICKING THE GLASS!

BUT I WANT ICE CREAM.

THEN GO GET A JOB AND BUY SOME. THOSE MT. RAZZLEBERRYS ARE FOR KIDS ONLY!

PARENTS JUST DON'T GET IT.

22

WELL, TOPPY, LOOKS LIKE I HAD YOU DRY-CLEANED FOR NOTHING.

THANKS FOR GIVING THEM A PIECE OF MY MIND!

CHEER UP, SQUIDWARD. WE WON YOU THIS PRIZE AT SKEE-BALL.

AND IT ONLY COST US $200 IN TOKENS!

A TOY CLARINET? WOW! THANKS, FELLAS!

HEY, YA KNOW, MY KID WON ME THIS KEY CHAIN THAT PLAYS REAL PIANO SOUND EFFECTS.

AND MY KID LEFT HIS EMPTY SODA BOTTLE.

GOOFY, GOOFY, GOOBER, GOOBER, YEAH!

LOOKS LIKE SQUIDWARD FINALLY GOT THAT SYMPHONY HE WANTED!

THE END

Puzzled with Patrick

It's me, Patrick. You like doing stuff? Tricky stuff? **HARD** stuff? That's great, because I need all the help I can get!

Tasty

Kraby Pattys!

Can you unscramble these letters to find something tasty to eat?

Yum, PIES!

B A B Y K R   T A T   P I E S

Which Way Now?

I have to get to SpongeBob's Pineapple house real quick! Can you help me find the way?

a
b
c
d

Did you do it? Me Neither!

Odd One Out

Which SpongeBob picture is the odd one out?

1.   2.
3.   4.
5.   6.

Yes, it's 2, the one where his shoelace is undone.

24

All Shook Up
Can you draw one?

Spot the Difference
Look hard at these two party photos.
Can you spot what's different?

1.

2.

*Even I can do this.
Here's my drawing!*

*Yup! I took photo 1 at last
year's Christmas party and
photo 2 at this year's.*

SpongeBob SquareWord
Can you find these Bikini Bottom words in the word square?

NAUTICAL

UNSINKABLE

WATERLOGGED

ABSORBENT

SEAWORTHY

DRENCHED

BARNACLES

SAILORIFIC

T	H	E	S	E
B	T	E	P	G
U	R	F	S	L
B	I	F	T	Y
W	O	R	D	S

*Did you find them?
THESE is on the top line and WORDS
is on the bottom. Easy, huh?*

Story and art: Carl Greenblatt. Colour: SnoCone Studios. SpongeBob SquarePants created by Stephen Hillenburg

END

PLANKTON'S PLAN

The micro-menace that is Sheldon Plankton has just one aim in his power-seeking little life.

Doing acts of kindness?

Finding peace?

Spreading happiness?

NO!

No, his aim is to ruin Mr Eugene Krabs. Plankton won't give up until he's put the Krusty Krab out of business and staged a Fast-Food **takeover** with his Chum Bucket set-up. The only way he'll do it is to steal the Krusty Krab's mega-successful recipe for Krabby Patties.

Once he tried to take over the Krusty Krab Fry cook's brain. When you know that the Fry cook in question is SpongeBob SquarePants, you'll see why that wasn't **ever** going to work.

At last, Plankton's got hold of the Krabby Patty recipe book. Can you help him crack the secret code and write the recipe?

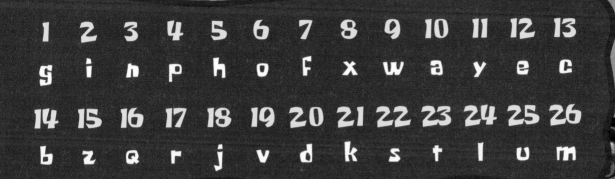

1	2	3	4	5	6	7	8	9	10	11	12	13
g	i	n	p	h	o	F	x	w	a	y	e	c

14	15	16	17	18	19	20	21	22	23	24	25	26
b	z	q	r	j	v	d	k	s	t	l	u	m

SECRET RECIPE

To make Krabby Patties you need:

200g of: 2 23 22   10   22 12 13 17 12 23

I t s a   s e c r e t

25ml of: 21 3 6 9 3   6 3 24 11   23 6   26 12

k n o w n   o n l y   t o   m e

100g of: 2 26   3 6 23   23 12 24 24 2 3 1

i'm   n o t   t e l l i n g

a pinch of: 9 6 25 24 20 3 23   11 6 25

w o u l d n't   y o u

24 2 21 12   23 6   21 3 6 9

l i k e   t o   k n o w

SpongeBob SquarePants

DINNER AT SANDY'S

MEOW! MEOW! HISS!

WHAT IS IT, GARY? A SEA BEAR?

A MONSTER?

A DENTIST?

OH, IT'S JUST THE MAILMAN!

STOP CHASING HIM, GARY!

WOW! AN INVITATION TO DINNER AT SANDY'S! WAIT'LL I TELL PATRICK!

Story: David Lewman. Pencils: Gregg Shigiel. Inks: Jeff Albrecht. Colour: SnoCone Studios. Letters: Comicraft. SpongeBob SquarePants created by Stephen Hillenburg.

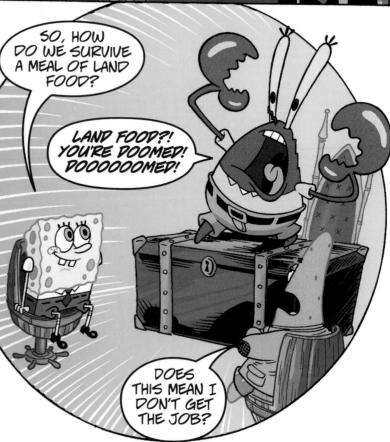

BIKINI BOTTOM STYLE

They do things differently in Bikini Bottom – *very* differently.

Dressing-up Bikini Bottom Style

Take your partners Bikini Bottom Style

Yoga Bikini Bottom Style

Disco Dancing Bikini Bottom Style

Having a Shave Bikini Bottom Styl

Horse Riding Bikini Bottom Style

A Christmas Tree Bikini Bottom Style

Sleepwalking Bikini Bottom Style

Hide and Seek Bikini Bottom Style

Fine Dining Bikini Bottom Style

Basketball Bikini Bottom Style

SpongeBob SquarePants

Cereal Baddie

BREAKFAST TIME!

Yes!

My very own cereal-bowl caddy!

Hang on, my new buddy, as I pour our cereal in...

...and add our milk!

Oh, this is going to be the best breakfast ever!

Pat! Pat!

DIG IN!

THE END

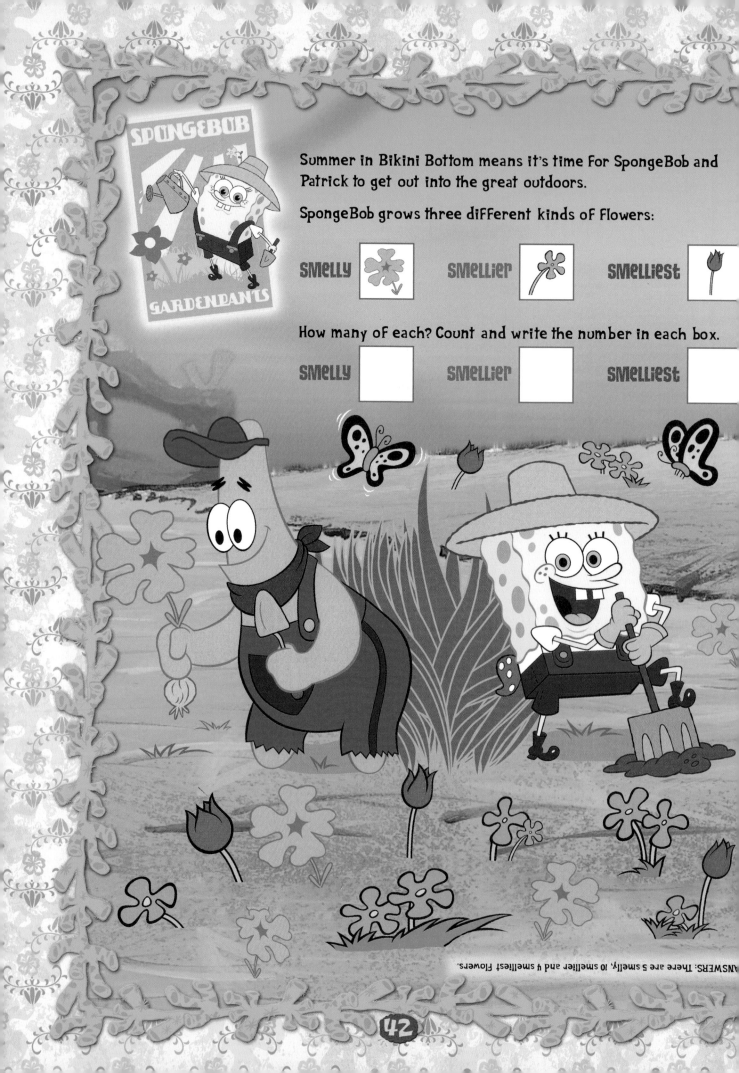

Summer in Bikini Bottom means it's time for SpongeBob and Patrick to get out into the great outdoors.

SpongeBob grows three different kinds of flowers:

SMELLY   SMELLIER   SMELLIEST

How many of each? Count and write the number in each box.

SMELLY   SMELLIER   SMELLIEST

Can you dig it? These pictures look the same, but there are **6 things** that are different in picture 2. Can you spot them all?

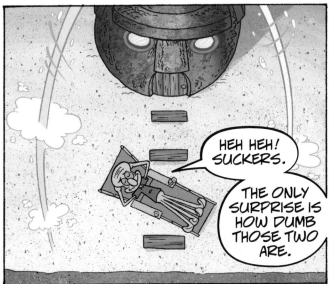

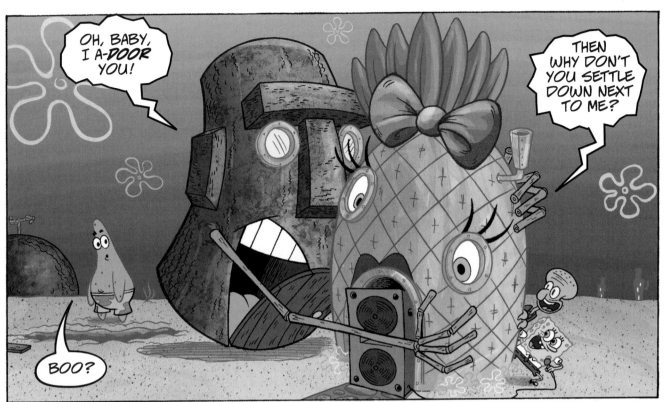

THE END

51

SpongeBob SmartyPants

I'M WITH THE DUMMY

SpongeBob SmartyPants got **2** of these questions right (3 and 8). Mind you, they *were* both about him ... Can you do better? Check out your score - and your prize - on page **53**.

① **What is Mr Krabs' First name? Is it:**

a) Eugene   b) Hygiene   c) Margarine

② **Karen is a computer. Who is she married to?**

a) Patrick   b) Plankton   c) Pearl

③ **Who is SpongeBob's teacher at the Bikini Bottom Boating School?**

a) Mrs Prof   b) Miss Chief   c) Mrs Puff

④ **Squidward Tentacles lives in Easter Island Toe:**

a) TRUE   b) FALSE

5 The Krusty Krab is an old:

a) shipwreck   b) lobster pot   c) treasure chest

6 Patrick Star lives at 120 Conch Street:

a) TRUE   b) FALSE

7 How many tentacles does Squidward Tentacles have?

a) 6   b) 8   c) 4

8 What colour underpants does SpongeBob wear?

a) red   b) white   c) black

Diploma

Score 1 point for each correct answer.

POINTS	PRIZE
8	one DAY jellyfishing with Patrick
5-7	one WEEK jellyfishing with Patrick
0-4	one MONTH jellyfishing with Patrick

ANSWERS: 1. a, Eugene. 2. b, Plankton. 3. c, Mrs Puff. 4. False, it's Easter Island Head. 5. b, lobster pot. 6. true. 7. a. 8. b, white.

53

Story: David Lewman. Pencils: Vince Deporter. Inks: Jeff Albrecht. Colour: SnoCone Studios. Lettering: Comicraft. *SpongeBob SquarePants* created by Stephen Hillenburg.

THE END

More Puzzled with Patrick

Me again. You still like doing stuff? Good, because here's some more stuff to do.

Yup, it's the one I just ate. *BURP*

Krabby Patty Line-up

Which Krabby Patty is missing?

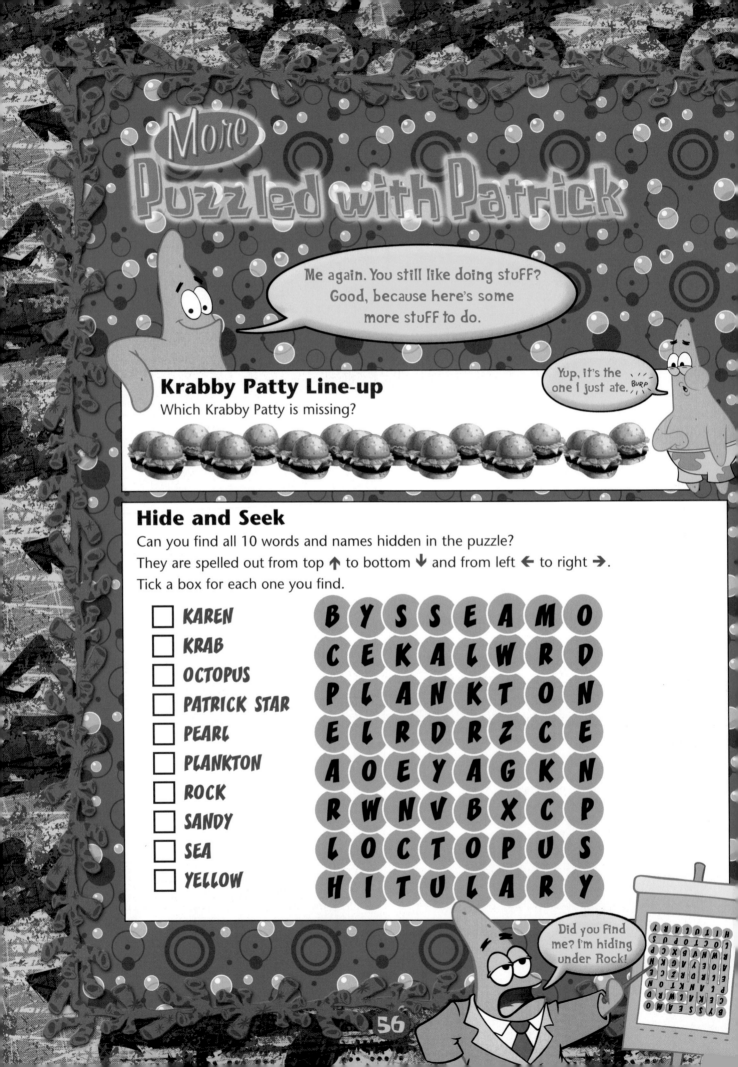

Hide and Seek

Can you find all 10 words and names hidden in the puzzle?

They are spelled out from top ↑ to bottom ↓ and from left ← to right →.

Tick a box for each one you find.

- [ ] **KAREN**
- [ ] **KRAB**
- [ ] **OCTOPUS**
- [ ] **PATRICK STAR**
- [ ] **PEARL**
- [ ] **PLANKTON**
- [ ] **ROCK**
- [ ] **SANDY**
- [ ] **SEA**
- [ ] **YELLOW**

```
B Y S S E A M O
C E K A L W R D
P L A N K T O N
E L R D R Z C E
A O E Y A G K N
R W N V B X C P
L O C T O P U S
H I T U L A R Y
```

Did you find me? I'm hiding under Rock!

56

Grid-locked

Use a black felt-tip to fill in the squares using the letter-and-number code to reveal my painting. Can you guess its name?

b3 d1 c4 a1 a3 e2 c2 b1 a4 c1
e3 e4 d2 c3 d4 a2 b4 e1 d3 b2

	a	b	c	d	e
1					
2					
3					
4					

I know! P is for Pants and S is for Square. It's for PantsSponge SquareBob!

Message for P.S.

I just got a message to give to *P.S.* But who's that?

It's called Night in Bikini Bottom.

Patrick's Paintings

Which of my paintings is different?

a.   b.   c.   d.   e.

It's c. I just did it, so the paint's still wet!

Code

Can you use the code to read my message?

H R C N T A E I

That makes two of us!

Story: David Lewman. Pencils: Gregg Shigiel. Inks: Jeff Albrecht. Colour: SnoCone Studios. Lettering: Comicraft. SpongeBob SquarePants created by Stephen Hillenburg.

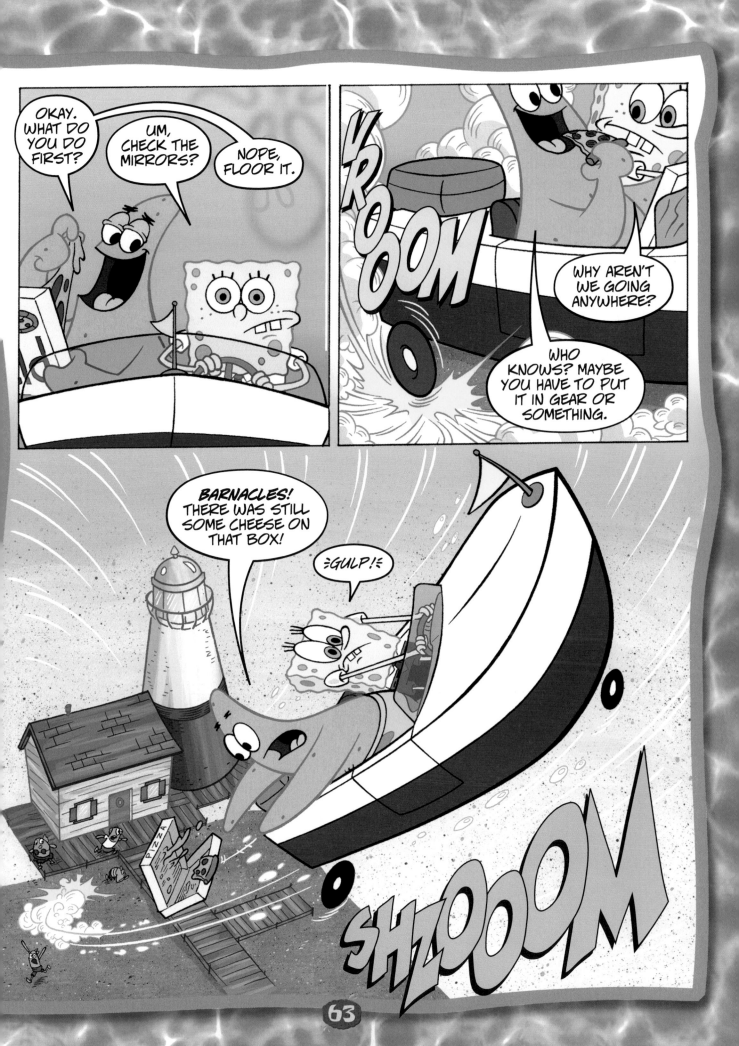

SPONGEBOB SQUAREART

SpongeBob has been painted **MANY** times by Bikini Bottom artists. Is it because he's strikingly handsome, charismatic ... or just that, being **SQUARE**, he fits nicely in a frame?

Here are some of the paintings of him that hang in the Bikini Bottom Gallery.

Now that's just **NOT** kind! It's nothing like me! Is it?

WORKS IN PROGRESS

Can you see **WHO** it is yet?
Draw your favourite Bikini Bottom resident, or - **YOU!**
Add a title for your picture, and your name.

BY

....

Did someone say **PAINTING?**
Here i am, ready and ... err ... ready!

Story: David Lewman. Pencils: Vince Deporter. Inks: Jeff Albrecht. Colour: SnoCone Studios. Lettering: Comicraft. SpongeBob SquarePants created by Stephen Hillenburg.

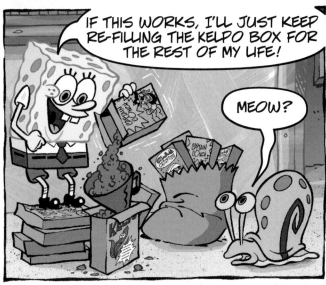